Friends in Nature

Discover Earth's Amazing Ecosystems

Marina Ruiz

LAURENCE KING

We live in a world bursting with LIVING THINGS.

Some are HUGE and MAJESTIC, like blue whales.

Some are so tiny, they're practically INVISIBLE, like microbes.

There are pine trees that have been
alive for THOUSANDS of years
and mayflies that will
only live for ONE DAY.

Some living things, like fruit bats,
fly EPIC distances every year,
while others, like moles, rarely
venture aboveground.

Our differences are INFINITE, but there's something
we all have in common: We need each other.

Can you imagine a world where you had
to do everything by yourself? It's pretty
impossible. The truth is, everyone needs
a little help from someone or something.

A FRIEND when you're lonely,
    a HELPING HAND with a heavy load,
        or someone to share a SECRET with . . .

            for all these things,
            we need others.

But it isn't just people like you and me who need each other. Look around—what other FRIENDSHIPS can you see?

Will the squirrel visit its favorite TREE today?

Will the birds find a comfy nook to NEST in?

If you listen carefully, you might hear busy bees buzzing. What could they need?

Singing and humming, their tiny wings flapping,
bees fly great distances for a snack and a drink.
For honeybees, there is no treat as delicious as
a sip of sweet nectar and a nibble of POLLEN.

Honeybees
love the sweet
scent of almond
tree blossoms.

While they are feeding,
honeybees transport pollen
from flower to flower, helping
the plants to reproduce.

This process is called POLLINATION.

Since most plants cannot move, they
need a little help from their winged
friends to carry their pollen around.

It isn't just bees that pollinate flowers. The SHAPE, COLOR, and SMELL of a flower will attract different types of pollinators.

Butterflies like calendula flowers because they provide a useful landing pad.

Flies love the rotting scent of chocolate lily flowers.

Nocturnal moths prefer flowers with white petals and strong scents like honeysuckle.

And insects aren't the only creatures with a sweet tooth! Each ECOSYSTEM has its own pollinators . . .

The south coast of Western Australia is home to the honey possum, one of the smallest marsupials in the world. Its diet consists entirely of POLLEN and NECTAR!

Using its LONG TONGUE, the honey possum mops up pollen from inside flowers. While feeding, its furry face gets covered in pollen, which it carries on to its next snack stop.

Banksia flower

Honey possum

Reaching inside long tube-shaped
flowers can be tricky, but not for
the sword-billed hummingbird.
Its BEAK is longer than its body!

Sword-billed
hummingbird

Curuba
flower

The saguaro cacti in the Sonoran Desert bloom
after dark to attract NOCTURNAL POLLINATORS.
They've become a favorite stop for bats
on their summer migration journey.

Lesser
long-nosed
bat

Saguaro
cactus

Once the plants have been pollinated,
they'll be able to start making SEEDS.

Seeds are little pods that contain the beginning of a new plant's life.

To find the perfect place to grow, plants have come up with some clever designs for their seeds that allow them to spread FAR AND WIDE.

Maple tree

Lime tree

Dandelions

Some have little WINGS that spin and spiral in the air.

Some are fluffy and light, and when the wind blows,

WHOOOOSH!

They float and glide away.

Some catch onto your clothes or animal fur with LITTLE HOOKS and hitch a ride.

Fox

Burdock

Some of them even explode . . .

BOOM!

They shoot their seeds out of little pods.

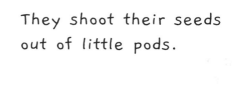

Squirting cucumber

But sometimes, having a good FRIEND to do the job might be just what you need . . .

Eurasian jay

Many animals love to eat SEEDS, which form a very important part of their diet. Once their tummies are full, some animals will hide seeds for winter, when there won't be as much food around.

Magpie

Nutcracker

Squirrel

Mouse

Crow

Often, the animals forget where they have buried these seeds.
OOOPS!
And some of them will sprout and grow into new trees.

Some plants cover their seeds in colorful jackets, creating DELICIOUS FRUIT!

Badger

The animals who eat the fruit carry the seeds in their bellies, until they eventually come out in their POOP.

The poop acts as a natural compost in which the seeds can grow.

Fruits and seeds are not only for small animals to enjoy. Plants in larger ecosystems need BIGGER FRIENDS to spread their seeds . . .

Below the canopy of the Congo rainforests in central Africa, plants compete for LIGHT, WATER, and NUTRIENTS. Finding space to grow isn't an easy business. Thankfully, animals are here to help!

Lowland gorilla

Lowland gorillas spend much of their time in jungle clearings. The seeds they scatter around in their poop will get plenty of light to help them GROW.

Forest elephants walk long distances every day. And while doing so, they spread tree seeds many miles away from the parent trees.

African forest elephant

Thanks to the elephants, new trees will grow. However, when it comes to transportation, you cannot beat . . .

WINGS! As the skies grow darker, a symphony of screeches and rustling fills the air. It's time for the straw-colored fruit bats to take charge of the night shift.

Straw-colored fruit bat

They set out at sunset, looking for their favorite treat: JUICY FRUIT!

They often venture beyond the border of the forest, scattering seeds in their poop as they travel.

In October, something extraordinary happens—the bats embark on the grandest mammal migration in Africa. Their destination? Kasanka National Park in Zambia. Up to TEN MILLION BATS gather in the forest, roosting and feeding until December.

Masuku fruit

During their journey, spanning hundreds of miles over vast savannas, the bats spread THOUSANDS OF SEEDS, some of which will grow into TREES.

Trees are scarce in the savanna, but there are plenty of big, hungry herbivores around. They love to feast on acacias, so these trees have had to make some special friends to avoid getting NIBBLED!

Acacias are home to bustling armies of ants. They live inside the hollow thorns on the trees and feed on delicious NECTAR made at the base of the leaves.

Acacia

Giraffe

But how can such tiny bodyguards defend a tree against animals so much bigger than them?

Acacia ant

When danger looms, they all jump into action, STINGING anyone who dares to take a bite!

Elephant

There's a place these large animals love to visit at the end of a hard day of walking and grazing . . .

What's better than a long bath and a sip of cool water on a scorching hot day? Why, a SPA TREATMENT, of course!

Have you ever wondered why egrets follow elephants around?

Egret

Elephant

Giraffe

Oxpecker

Or why giraffes, zebras, and hippos often wander with a flock of oxpeckers on their backs?

Parasites are miniscule creatures that live on bigger animals, and they can make them feel ITCHY and SICK. Fortunately, parasites are a tasty snack for birds! So, while the egrets and oxpeckers are enjoying dinner, their friends are given a good cleaning, leaving them itch-free and healthy.

Gazelle

Zebra

Hippo

But birds are not the only cleaners in nature . . .

Even in the vast OCEAN DEPTHS, there are pesky parasites causing trouble. They hang around in the mouths, gills, and fins of sea creatures.

Turtle

Barracuda

In the vibrant coral reefs of Australia, fish and turtles line up, eagerly waiting to get a good clean. They hover in one spot while little cleaner wrasses nibble away dead skin, scales, and parasites—what a FANTASTIC FEAST!

Believe it or not, wrasses will even venture inside a **shark's** mouth to eat any morsels of food leftover from its last meal! But don't worry, sharks won't harm their helpful pals.

Cleaner wrasse

Gray reef shark

Reef manta ray

Not everyone is as lucky, though. So, when sharks start to feel hungry, for most fish it's time to HIDE!

As **sharks** and other predators hunt for food, smaller creatures **TEAM UP** to stay safe in the reef.

Let's meet the clever **clown fish** and its best friend, the **sea anemone**!

The anemone's tentacles are **TOXIC** to most, but not to clown fish. And a safe home for the clown fish means dinner for the anemone . . .

Clown fish

Sea anemone

As the clown fish wriggle inside for safety, they lure small fish in, which the anemone can sting and eat.

Another peculiar friendship is the one between
gobies and **pistol shrimp.**

The goby gets a comfy
house, thanks to the shrimp's
amazing DIGGING skills . . .

Goby

Pistol
shrimp

. . . while the shrimp relies on
the goby's amazing EYESIGHT
to watch out for danger.

Occasionally, they might even share a
meal together! But these aren't the only
ways to keep SAFE in the reef . . .

There might be creatures hiding around these rocks. Can you spot them?

Come a bit closer.
Can you see them NOW?

Mimic octopuses are masters of DISGUISE. They can blend into the background by changing their COLOR, TEXTURE, and PATTERN in a fraction of a second.

Mimic octopus

Others, such as the little **decorator crab**, might need some help from their pals. A little seaweed here, a couple of shells there—perfect!

Decorator crab

Anemones

Boxer crab

Oh, yes . . . and why not use some stinging **anemones** as pom-poms to keep predators at bay? Anemones will get a sweet ride and get to munch some plankton on the way.

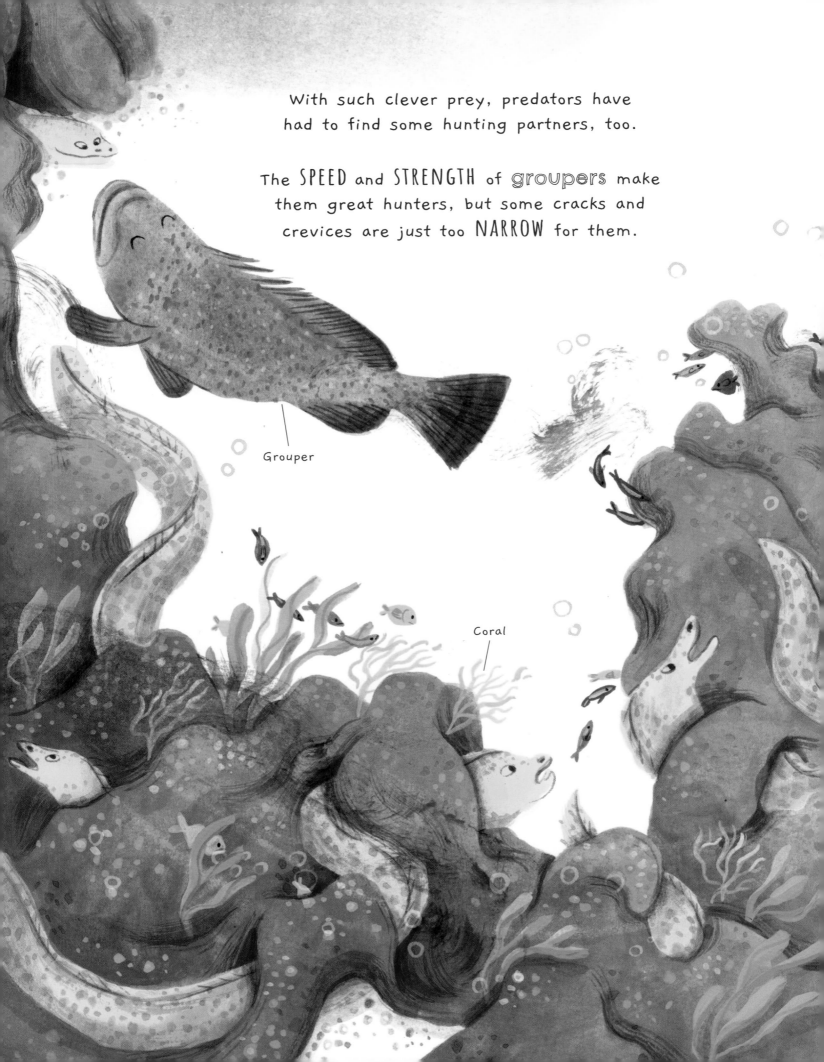

With such clever prey, predators have
had to find some hunting partners, too.

The SPEED and STRENGTH of groupers make
them great hunters, but some cracks and
crevices are just too NARROW for them.

Grouper

Coral

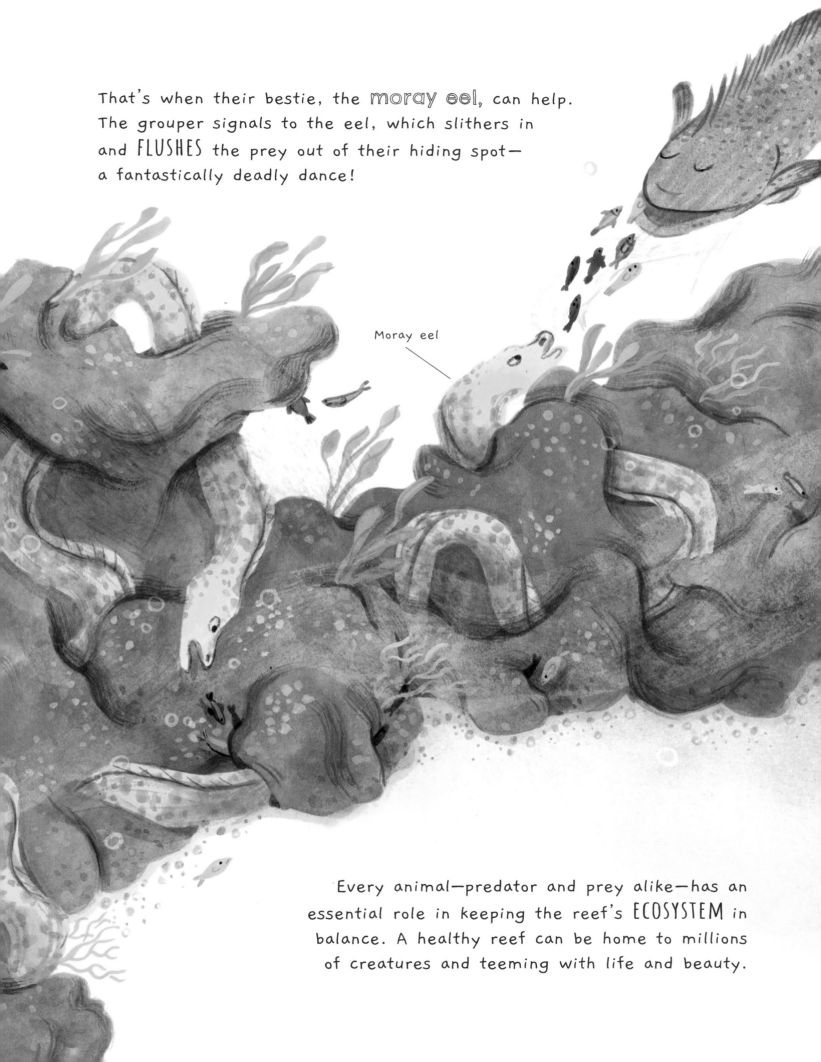

That's when their bestie, the moray eel, can help.
The grouper signals to the eel, which slithers in
and FLUSHES the prey out of their hiding spot—
a fantastically deadly dance!

Moray eel

Every animal—predator and prey alike—has an
essential role in keeping the reef's ECOSYSTEM in
balance. A healthy reef can be home to millions
of creatures and teeming with life and beauty.

Creating a home at sea is tricky with all the swirling and swaying water. Can you imagine drifting off to sleep and waking up on the other side of town?

Sea otters have found their perfect home in KELP FORESTS.

Sea otter

This seaweed anchors them while they rest and attracts otters' best-loved meal: sea urchins.

Sea urchin

Urchins love kelp, too—they enjoy devouring its ROOTS!

By keeping urchin numbers in check, otters PROTECT the seaweed forest and the thousands of species that find shelter and food in it.

Salmon

Kelp

One of these species is salmon. They live in and around kelp forests for part of their life.

Salmon

Once salmon reach maturity, they begin an EPIC JOURNEY back to the rivers where they were born, and here they will lay their EGGS.

Salmon swim THOUSANDS of miles to get to calmer rivers.

The salmon LEAP and TUMBLE through rough waters. It's not an easy journey!

Wolf

Bald eagle

Thousands of salmon battle against the current, diving across pools and SOARING through waterfalls.

Flickers of silver catch the eye of predators that gather along the riverbanks. Birds dart underwater, and bears catch them with their mouths and claws.

Grizzly bear

But still, thousands of salmon will make it upstream.

Surrounded by forest, salmon find the perfect
place to SPAWN. Here, they reunite with
their long-lost friends, the trees.

Conifer

Seagull

Fox

Salmon

Trees and salmon spend most of their lives apart, but their RELATIONSHIP and DEPENDENCE on each other shape forests and rivers, as well as many other species that make these places their home.

Tree roots hold the soil, filtering the water to make it pure for salmon to lay their eggs in.

Wolf

Crow

Fungi

Worms

Most salmon will die after spawning, but their remains will feed many animals. Their bones will FERTILIZE the soil, helping trees, plants, and fungi grow stronger. Every part of the fish shapes the ecosystem.

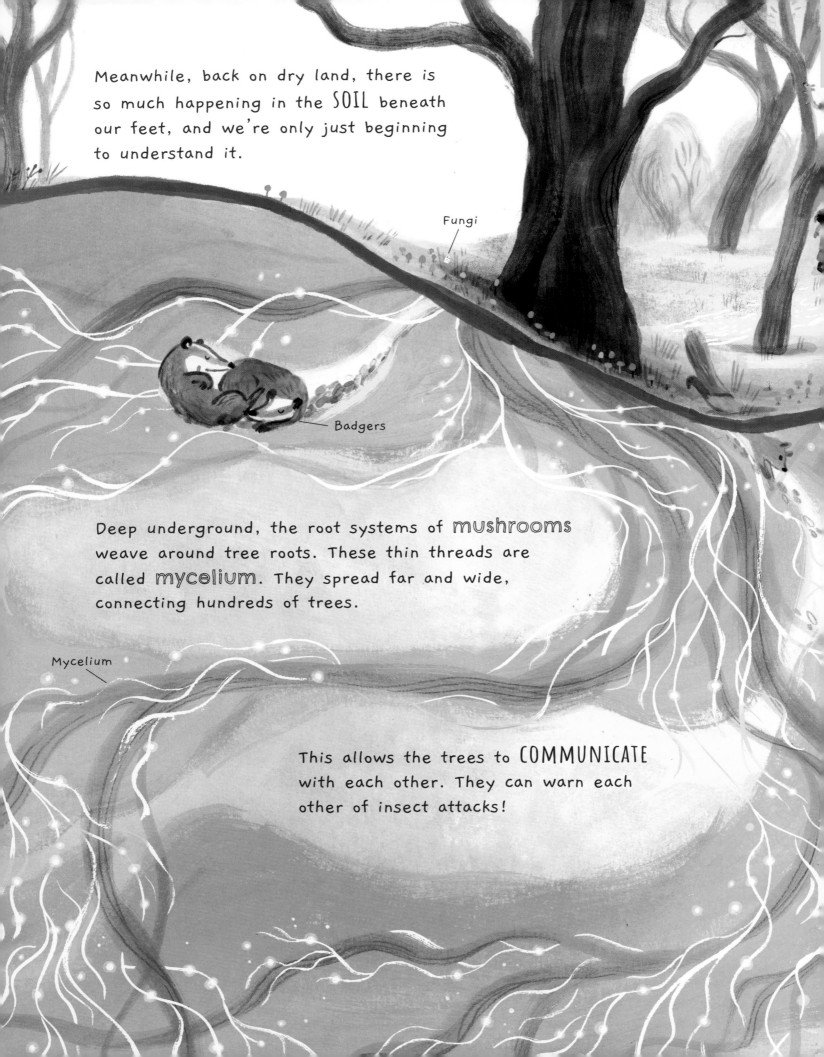

Meanwhile, back on dry land, there is so much happening in the SOIL beneath our feet, and we're only just beginning to understand it.

Fungi

Badgers

Deep underground, the root systems of mushrooms weave around tree roots. These thin threads are called mycelium. They spread far and wide, connecting hundreds of trees.

Mycelium

This allows the trees to COMMUNICATE with each other. They can warn each other of insect attacks!

Fungi also help trees absorb nutrients and keep the soil healthy. In return, they get FOOD and ENERGY from trees.

Rabbits

Squirrels

Mycelium

There are also animals to be found here. Who can you see scuttling around underground?

Fox

Many animals make their homes among the trees.

A woodpecker uses its strong, pointed beak
to hammer a nesting hole into the trunk.

Woodpecker

Hare

Barn owl

After using it, the woodpecker leaves
the hole for other animals, such as owls
and squirrels, to make their home.

Mice

Moles

Moles prefer living under the roots.
They dig amazing BURROWS connected
with tunnels—it's like a whole
neighborhood hidden underground!

Some birds prefer to use the branches as their quarters. They build elaborate NESTS using little sticks and moss. High above the ground, they're safe from many predators.

Blackbird

Even the leaves of trees are used as homes. Tent-making bats chew on leaves, shaping them to make a cozy NOOK.

Honduran white bats

So much life depends on trees for shelter!

We need trees, too!

Look around you. How many things are made of wood?

The CHAIR where you sit,

the BED where you sleep,

the GUITAR you use to play your favorite songs.

Wood can be used for so many things, including making PAPER!

Trees offer SHADE on a hot day and shelter when a storm rolls in.

They produce OXYGEN, making the air good to breathe.

They give us FRUIT and NUTS to eat.

And every part of the tree, from its roots to its leaves, can be used to make MEDICINE!

So when you walk through a forest or a city park, don't forget to look up and thank the trees for all they do for us.

Trees need US, too!

A long time ago, huge areas of our planet were
covered in lush forests. As we chopped down trees for
their wood and to make space for farmland, roads,
and buildings, many of these forests DISAPPEARED.

But we can HELP trees now!
We can start by planting
saplings and taking care of
the forests we still have.

Remember—everything is
connected, so it is not just the
trees we need to care for . . .

We need to protect the bees that POLLINATE the trees' flowers, the animals that SPREAD their seeds, the fungi that FERTILIZE their soil, and the insects that PROTECT them from attack.

Our world is like a large, beautiful tapestry, in which every species is a thread interwoven with all the others, holding the piece together. We are ALL interconnected, from the ecosystems on our doorsteps to those far beyond.

Apple trees rely on bees to POLLINATE
their flowers and make seeds,
which feed the birds
throughout the year.

Far away in African jungles, trees
count on elephants to SPREAD their seeds,
who need egrets to keep them free
of parasites, while the egrets
rely on parasites for FOOD.

Salmon need trees to CLEAN the water
where they lay their eggs,
and bears rely on the salmon
for food, giving them ENERGY
to get through the long
winter months.

Bears FERTILIZE the soil with their poop,
which helps fungi grow stronger.
These fungi help trees to GROW and
COMMUNICATE, maintaining a healthy
forest for all the creatures who live in it.

From tiny bees to mighty bears and from cleaner wrasse
to you and me, every living thing has a role to play—
ensuring harmony in nature's great tapestry.

WAYS TO HELP BIODIVERSITY

You can help keep nature's beautiful tapestry healthy. For that, you don't need to dive into the ocean or hike across jungles—remember, everything is interconnected! Here are some ways you can encourage biodiversity right on your doorstep.

Build a bug hotel

Just like us, insects and spiders need homes! Different natural materials will attract different insect guests. For a ladybug hotel, you will need pine cones, twigs, and dry leaves. For a roof, you could use two old tiles or small wooden planks.

- Find a sheltered spot in your yard or school playground.

- Bundle the pine cones together so that their scales interlock. Fill the gaps with dry leaves and twigs.

- Finally, place the roof on top to keep the rain out.

Grow flowers for pollinating insects

As you've seen, moths, butterflies, bees, and flies need nectar for survival, and their role as pollinators is essential for a healthy ecosystem. We can help them by planting pollinator-friendly plants on our balcony or in our yard. Lavender, thyme, and marjoram are excellent options, and they produce some very pretty flowers!

Take a nature walk

Go to a local park or woodland (if you have one nearby) with your family, and make a note of all the different types of wildlife you spot. Can you see any animals? Which insects can you find? Why not keep a nature journal to write down – or even sketch! – the different forms of life that you see on your walk!

GLOSSARY

BIODIVERSITY All the different forms of life that you find living in one area. Together, they form an ecosystem.

ECOSYSTEM An area where plants, animals, and other things, including weather and land, exist together in harmony.

HERBIVORE An animal that mainly eats plants.

MARSUPIAL A mammal that carries and feeds its young in a pouch on its stomach.

MICROBES Tiny, simple forms of life.

MIGRATION A journey from one home to another.

PLANKTON A group of tiny creatures and plants that live in oceans and lakes.

PREDATORS Animals that hunt and eat other animals.

PREY Animals that are hunted by other animals for food.

SAPLING A young tree.

SAVANNA Dry grassland areas, usually flat and open.

SPAWN When fish, or other animals such as frogs, lay eggs.

TAPESTRY A type of art where many threads are woven onto fabric to create a picture.

To my mum and dad, for inspiring my love for
the living world. And to all those, big and small,
who take care of nature's big tapestry ~ M.R.

LAURENCE KING

LAURENCE KING
First published in the United States in 2025 by Laurence King

Text and illustrations copyright © Marina Ruiz 2025

ISBN: 978-1-510-23082-8

1 3 5 7 9 10 8 6 4 2

Printed in China

FSC
www.fsc.org
MIX
Paper | Supporting
responsible forestry
FSC® C104740

Laurence King
An imprint of Hachette Children's Group
Part of Hodder and Stoughton
Carmelite House
50 Victoria Embankment
London EC4Y 0DZ

The authorised representative in the EEA is Hachette Ireland, 8 Castlecourt Centre,
Dublin 15, D15 XTP3, Ireland (email: info@hbgi.ie)

An Hachette UK Company
www.hachette.co.uk
www.hachettechildrens.co.uk
www.laurenceking.com